What Is Hiding?

By Cheryl Jakab

Illustrated by Luke Jurevicius

What is hiding?
Can you see?

Where is it hiding?
What can it be?

Where is the spider?
Look and see.

I can see the spider.
It cannot hide from me!

Where is the caterpillar?

Look and see.

I can see the caterpillar.
It cannot hide from me!

Where is the lizard?
Look and see.

I can see the lizard.
It cannot hide from me!

Where is the moth?

Look and see.

I can see the moth.
It cannot hide from me!

Where is the ant?
Look and see.

12

I can see the ant.
It cannot hide from me!

Where is the frog?
Look and see.

I can see the frog.
It cannot hide from me!

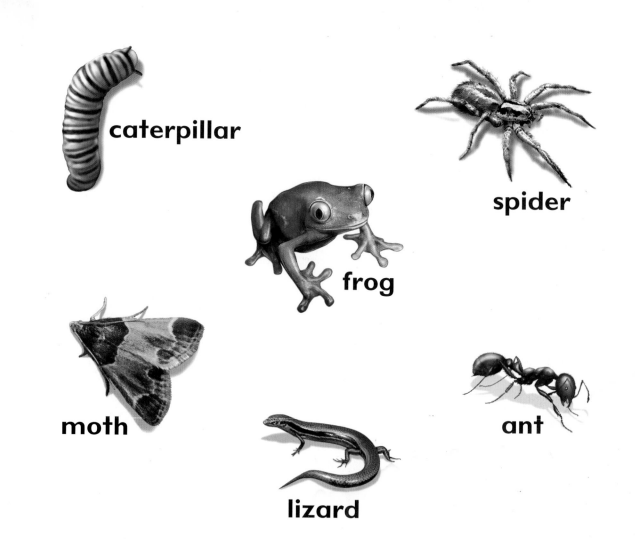

caterpillar

spider

frog

moth

lizard

ant